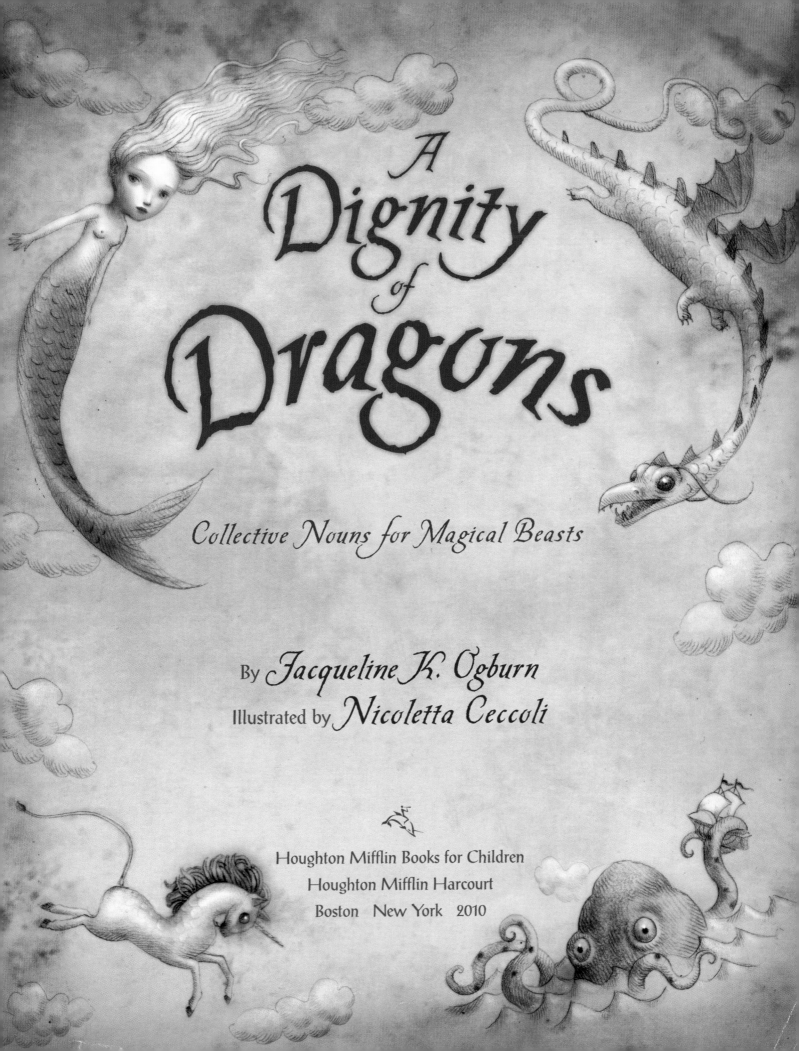

A Dignity of Dragons

Collective Nouns for Magical Beasts

By Jacqueline K. Ogburn

Illustrated by Nicoletta Ceccoli

Houghton Mifflin Books for Children

Houghton Mifflin Harcourt

Boston New York 2010

"Well, now that we have seen each other," said the Unicorn,

"if you'll believe in me, I'll believe in you. Is that a bargain?"

~ *Through the Looking-Glass* by Lewis Carroll

Everyone has heard of groups of animals— a pride of lions, a charm of hummingbirds, a school of fish. If you came upon magical beasts gathered together, what would you call them? Perhaps you would be lucky enough to see . . .

A blaze of fire-breathers

A torrent of water-dwellers

A dignity of dragons

A bolt of hippogriffs

A grapple of griffins

A riddle of sphinx

A flame of feng hwangs

A resurrection of phoenix

A flash of firebirds

A tsunami of sea monsters

A continent of kracken

A cresting of sea horses

A wave of sea serpents

A splash of mermaids

A flurry of yetis

An avalanche of abominable snowmen

A thicket of Bigfoots

An amazement of minotaurs

A pandemonium of fauns

A faculty of centaurs

A dazzlement of Quetzalcoatls

An arch of rainbow snakes

A judgment of kirin

A wisdom of
Chi'lin

A grace of unicorns

A storm of thunderbirds

A thundering of rocs

A vengeance of harpies

A tangle of gorgons

A chord of sirens

A confusion of chimeras

A roaring of manticores

A glare of cockatrice

A shifting of weres

A slinking of were-jaguars

A cleverness of
were-foxes

A howling of werewolves

A rumble of were-bears

Abominable Snowmen (Tibet and Nepal) This is the European name for the giant humanoids that live in the Himalayan Mountain ranges, which the locals call the yeti. They are covered with white fur and have large pointed heads. Many twentieth-century European climbers, including the party of Sir Edmund Hillary, have reported seeing their huge footprints.

Bigfoots (United States and Canada) Also known as Sasquatch, these large (seven feet tall or taller) fur-covered humanoids generally live in the northwestern forests. The Lakota call them "Big Elder Brother." They are known to steal salmon from fishermen and leave behind a big stench as well as the famous big footprints.

Centaurs (Greece) Centaurs have the legs and body of horses and the torso and head of humans. They are very wise—and many are great teachers—being especially learned in medicine and the arts. The centaur Chiron was the teacher of several heroes, including Jason and Theseus.

Chi-lin (China) These unicorns have the body of a deer, legs of horse, and a coat of five colors. They frequently appear at the birth of sages, such as the one reported at the birth of Confucius. The Chi'lin is one of the four great spiritual creatures of Chinese culture, a being of gentleness and the bringer of good fortune.

Chimeras (Greece) Chimeras have two heads at the front—a lion's and a goat's—and a tail that ends in the head of a snake. They also breathe fire. The Greek hero Bellerophon killed a chimera while riding the winged horse Pegasus.

Cockatrice (Europe, Middle East) Cockatrice have the head and body of a rooster and the tail of a snake. They are so poisonous that a touch, breath, and even glance from one can kill. They are said to be hatched from roosters' eggs.

Dragons (Europe and Asia) European dragons are giant winged reptilian creatures that fly and breathe fire. They frequently guard hoards of treasure. While many are destructive, some European dragons have special wisdom. There are smaller breeds, such as wyrens and fire-drakes. Asian dragons have a snakelike body, tiger claws, and a lion head. Some can fly through the air. Asian dragons usually live under water, in rivers and seas. They are frequently the benefactors of humans, giving them the knowledge of writing and other gifts. Dragons are one of the great spiritual beings of China and the symbol of the emperor.

Fauns (Greece) Half human and half goat, with small horns and pointed ears, fauns are followers of the god Pan. They love to play music and dance, and are more polite than their relations the satyrs. Fauns are guardians of their native woodlands.

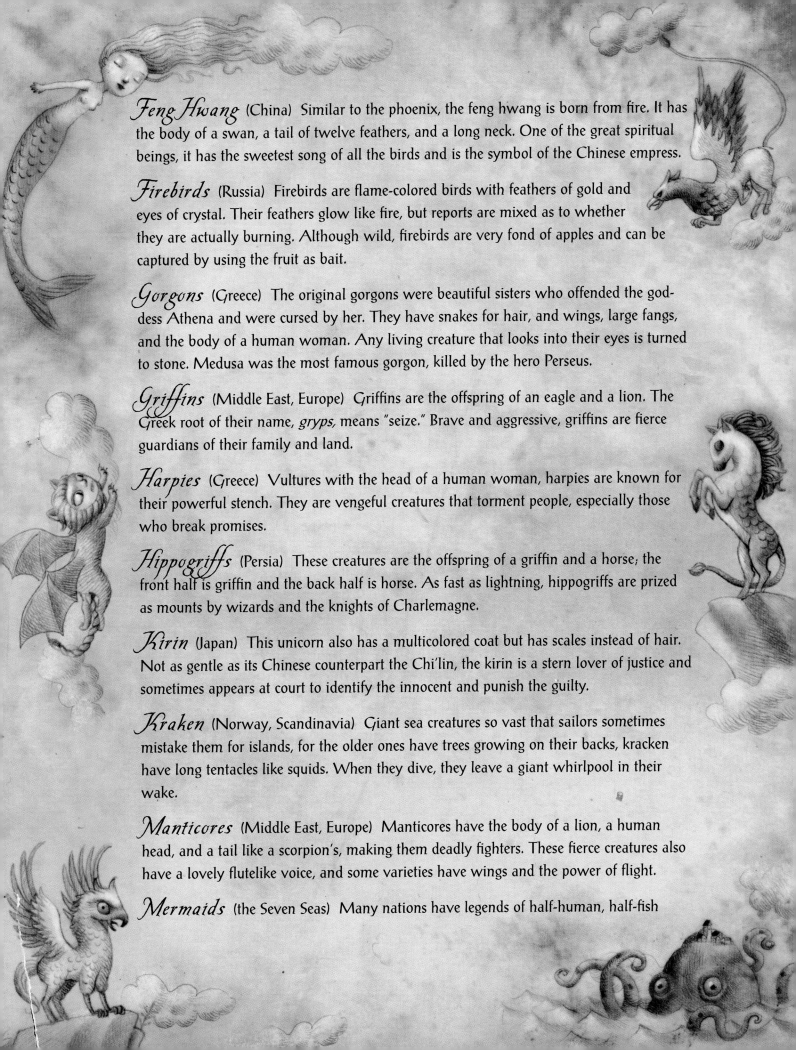

Feng Hwang (China) Similar to the phoenix, the feng hwang is born from fire. It has the body of a swan, a tail of twelve feathers, and a long neck. One of the great spiritual beings, it has the sweetest song of all the birds and is the symbol of the Chinese empress.

Firebirds (Russia) Firebirds are flame-colored birds with feathers of gold and eyes of crystal. Their feathers glow like fire, but reports are mixed as to whether they are actually burning. Although wild, firebirds are very fond of apples and can be captured by using the fruit as bait.

Gorgons (Greece) The original gorgons were beautiful sisters who offended the goddess Athena and were cursed by her. They have snakes for hair, and wings, large fangs, and the body of a human woman. Any living creature that looks into their eyes is turned to stone. Medusa was the most famous gorgon, killed by the hero Perseus.

Griffins (Middle East, Europe) Griffins are the offspring of an eagle and a lion. The Greek root of their name, *gryps,* means "seize." Brave and aggressive, griffins are fierce guardians of their family and land.

Harpies (Greece) Vultures with the head of a human woman, harpies are known for their powerful stench. They are vengeful creatures that torment people, especially those who break promises.

Hippogriffs (Persia) These creatures are the offspring of a griffin and a horse; the front half is griffin and the back half is horse. As fast as lightning, hippogriffs are prized as mounts by wizards and the knights of Charlemagne.

Kirin (Japan) This unicorn also has a multicolored coat but has scales instead of hair. Not as gentle as its Chinese counterpart the Chi'lin, the kirin is a stern lover of justice and sometimes appears at court to identify the innocent and punish the guilty.

Kraken (Norway, Scandinavia) Giant sea creatures so vast that sailors sometimes mistake them for islands, for the older ones have trees growing on their backs, kracken have long tentacles like squids. When they dive, they leave a giant whirlpool in their wake.

Manticores (Middle East, Europe) Manticores have the body of a lion, a human head, and a tail like a scorpion's, making them deadly fighters. These fierce creatures also have a lovely flutelike voice, and some varieties have wings and the power of flight.

Mermaids (the Seven Seas) Many nations have legends of half-human, half-fish

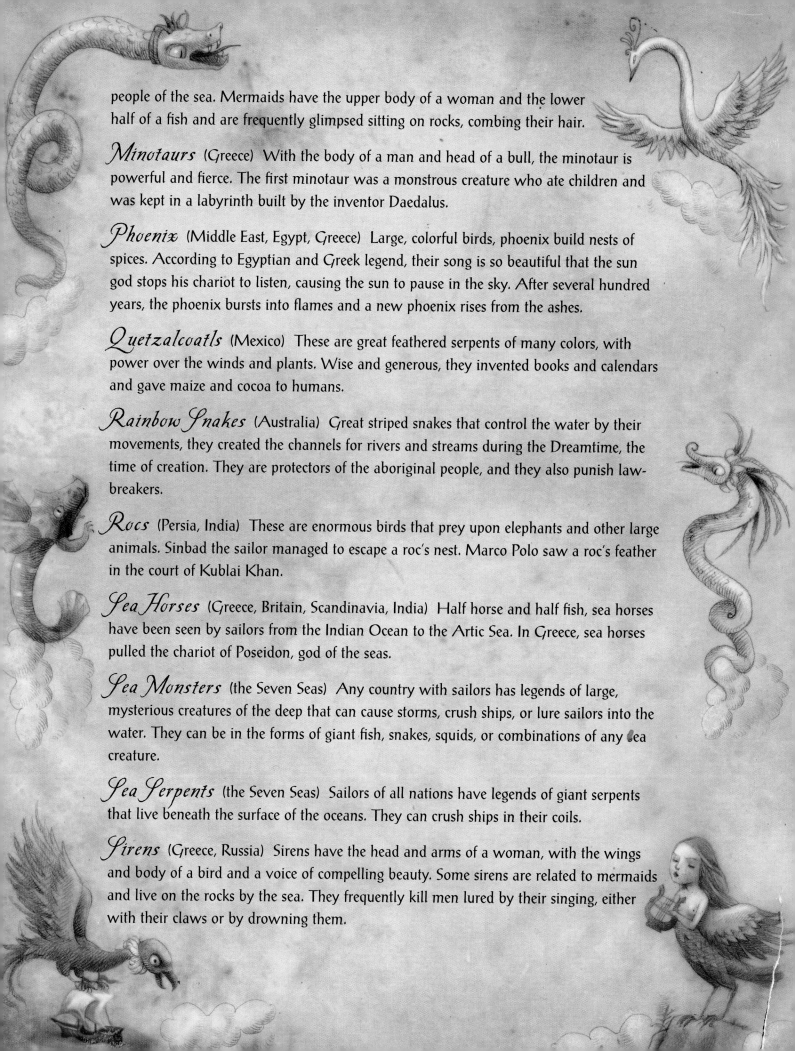

people of the sea. Mermaids have the upper body of a woman and the lower half of a fish and are frequently glimpsed sitting on rocks, combing their hair.

Minotaurs (Greece) With the body of a man and head of a bull, the minotaur is powerful and fierce. The first minotaur was a monstrous creature who ate children and was kept in a labyrinth built by the inventor Daedalus.

Phoenix (Middle East, Egypt, Greece) Large, colorful birds, phoenix build nests of spices. According to Egyptian and Greek legend, their song is so beautiful that the sun god stops his chariot to listen, causing the sun to pause in the sky. After several hundred years, the phoenix bursts into flames and a new phoenix rises from the ashes.

Quetzalcoatls (Mexico) These are great feathered serpents of many colors, with power over the winds and plants. Wise and generous, they invented books and calendars and gave maize and cocoa to humans.

Rainbow Snakes (Australia) Great striped snakes that control the water by their movements, they created the channels for rivers and streams during the Dreamtime, the time of creation. They are protectors of the aboriginal people, and they also punish law-breakers.

Rocs (Persia, India) These are enormous birds that prey upon elephants and other large animals. Sinbad the sailor managed to escape a roc's nest. Marco Polo saw a roc's feather in the court of Kublai Khan.

Sea Horses (Greece, Britain, Scandinavia, India) Half horse and half fish, sea horses have been seen by sailors from the Indian Ocean to the Artic Sea. In Greece, sea horses pulled the chariot of Poseidon, god of the seas.

Sea Monsters (the Seven Seas) Any country with sailors has legends of large, mysterious creatures of the deep that can cause storms, crush ships, or lure sailors into the water. They can be in the forms of giant fish, snakes, squids, or combinations of any sea creature.

Sea Serpents (the Seven Seas) Sailors of all nations have legends of giant serpents that live beneath the surface of the oceans. They can crush ships in their coils.

Sirens (Greece, Russia) Sirens have the head and arms of a woman, with the wings and body of a bird and a voice of compelling beauty. Some sirens are related to mermaids and live on the rocks by the sea. They frequently kill men lured by their singing, either with their claws or by drowning them.

Sphinx (Egypt, Middle East, Greece) Egyptian sphinx have the head of a man and body of a lion and are a symbol of royalty. Assyrian sphinx are the guardians of temples. Greek sphinx have the head of a woman, wings of an eagle, and body of a lion. A Greek sphinx held the city of Thebes hostage until Oedipus answered her riddle.

Thunderbirds (Native America) These gigantic birds create thunder with their wings, which are the length of two canoes, and flash lightning from their eyes. Intelligent and wrathful, they prey upon deer in the forests and plains and whales off the northwest coast.

Unicorns (Europe, Middle East) These creatures have the body of a horse, the beard of a goat, and a single horn growing from their forehead. Unicorns have healing powers and so have always been hunted for their medicinal horns. They can be fierce, but are fond of music and children.

Were-bears (Russia, Native America, Scandinavia) While all were-bears, who usually transform by night, are powerful and dangerous, the Russian and Native American forms can be protectors of a village or people as well as threats. The Norse berserkers were warriors who changed into bears in battle and felt no pain while fighting.

Were-fox (Japan) Many weres are people who turn into animals, but these are foxes, also called kitsune, who turn into people—mostly women. They can be helpful or troublesome, and sometimes marry human men who are unaware of their true nature.

Were-jaguars (South America) Were-jaguars are commonly depicted in the art of many pre-Columbian peoples. Among the Aztec, the strongest warriors were chosen to become were-jaguars and transformed by wrapping themselves in jaguar skins.

Weres (Worldwide) The word *were* is the general prefix for a shape-shifter, a creature with the ability to change from a human into an animal form and back again. Usually, their forms are fully human or fully animal instead of a mixture.

Werewolves (Europe) Werewolves must transform on the night of the full moon and return to human form by day. A person who survives a werewolf attack will turn into a werewolf at the next full moon. They have great healing ability, but can be killed by silver.

Yetis (Tibet and Nepal) Yetis are sometimes described as being more bearlike in shape than the abominable snowmen. The British newspaper the *Daily Mail* sponsored an expedition to find the yeti in 1954, and many mysterious footprints were photographed then.

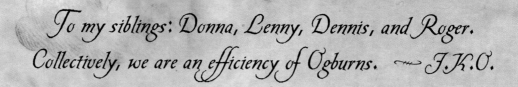

To my siblings: Donna, Lenny, Dennis, and Roger.
Collectively, we are an efficiency of Ogburns. ⟶ *J.K.O.*

A mio fratello Checco, bestia rara. ⟶ *N.C.*

Houghton Mifflin Books for Children is an imprint of Houghton Mifflin Harcourt Publishing Company.

www.hmhbooks.com

Decorated "E" on page 3 taken from *1000 Decorated Initials*,
published by The Pepin Press, www.pepinpress.com

The text of this book is set in Carmilla and Post Antiqua.
The illustrations are done in mixed media, including plasticine, acrylics, collage, and computer graphics.

Library of Congress Cataloging-in-Publication Data
Ogburn, Jacqueline K.
A dignity of dragons : collective nouns for magical beasts /
by Jacqueline K. Ogburn, Nicoletta Ceccoli; illustrated by Nicoletta Ceccoli.
p. cm.   ISBN 978-0-618-86254-2 (alk. paper)
1.   Animals, Mythical–Juvenile literature. 2.   English language–Collective nouns–Juvenile literature.
I. Ceccoli, Nicoletta. II. Title.   GR825.O44 2010   398.24'54–dc22   2009024165

Manufactured in Singapore
TWP 10 9 8 7 6 5 4 3 2 1